# THE GORILLA WHO WANTED TO DANCE

Written & Illustrated by
Linda Marchus

For all of my dancing gorillas (in order of appearance):
Rebecca, Bryce, Eli, Jason, Tony, Tara Rose, Ke'Shawn, Abigail and David.

One day in the jungle all snug in their trees,
The gorillas were napping, except for Louise.
When she heard a drum making a musical sound,
She put on her dance shoes and jumped to the ground.

Louise began moving her two chubby feet,
And then started rocking along with the beat.

She really was taking a mighty big chance.
Gorillas were strictly forbidden to dance.

"Stop!" roared the king. "You're breaking the rules.
Gorillas who dance always look like such fools.
I speak for us all when I tell you with pride,
Gorillas can't dance, it's not dignified.

"If you keep on dancing this outrageous way,
I'll command you to leave the gorillas today!"
Louise told the king, "If you really must know,
I'm not going to stop, so I'll just have to go.

"I'll feel very sad and miss everyone too,
But going away is the best thing to do.

Gorillas can dance and I'll prove it somehow.
I'll just have to find a new dance place for now."

Louise danced away to the drum's steady beat,
Till she came to a tree and two dangling feet.
A monkey sat pounding a drum with a stick.
"I'm a drummer," he said, "and my friends call me Rick."

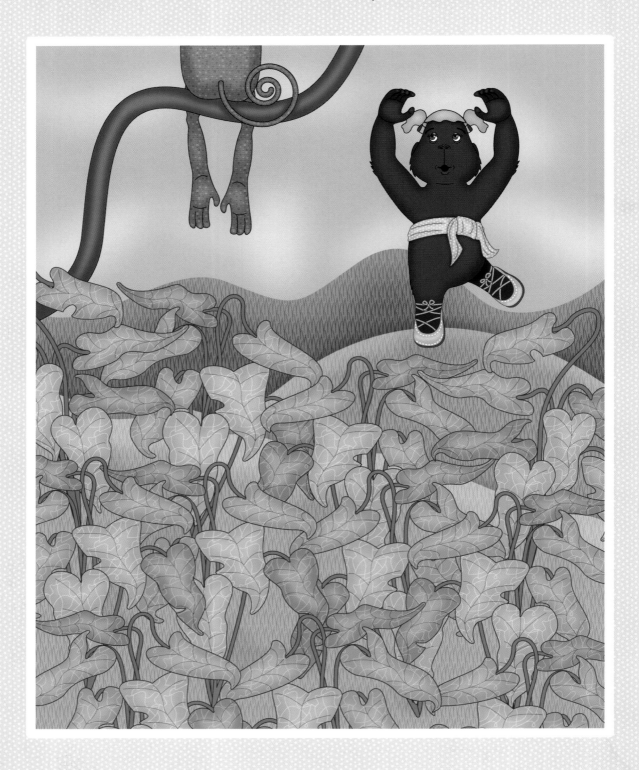

"Will you keep on playing your drum for me please?
The strong steady beat helps me dance," said Louise.
"I will," Rick replied, "it will be a delight."
Then a noise from the bush made them both jump with fright.

A be-bopping elephant boogied right by.
He circled around with his trunk held up high.
"I'm Alvin," he said, "and I dance really fine.
I make jazzy moves that are simply divine."

He strutted about as he swiveled his trunk.
He bumped poor Louise and they fell with a thunk.
They picked themselves up and continued to prance,
When a new jungle animal joined in their dance.

A giraffe tangoed by in a curious way.
His two gliding feet caused his long neck to sway.
He said, "My name's Biff and I really do try,
But my dancing is odd since I'm such a tall guy."

He took several steps, wobbled out of control,
Slipped to the ground and started to roll.
He rolled down a hill till he came to a stop,
Sprang to his feet and danced back to the top.

A lion who tapped was the last on the scene.
She click-clacked a snappy tap dancing routine.
"I'm Clarissa," she said. "I'm a fast tapping girl,
But my speed is a problem when I tap a twirl."

She wiggled her tummy and shimmied her bum.
She tip-tapped her feet to the beat of the drum.
When she started to twirl, she stumbled instead,
Then flipped upside-down and fell on her head.

The little troupe practiced with all of its might,
But no one was able to do their steps right.
When one of them boogied, another sashayed.
They made a hilarious dancing brigade.

One by one they improved at a nice steady rate.
By the end of the week their dancing was great.
"Now," said Louise, "we can have some real fun.
Let's put on a show and invite everyone."

With his trunk Alvin tooted a loud trumpet call,
"Come to our show, won't you come one and all?"

Louise and Clarissa made costumes to wear,
While Biff decorated the stage with great care.

Everyone came to the little dance show,

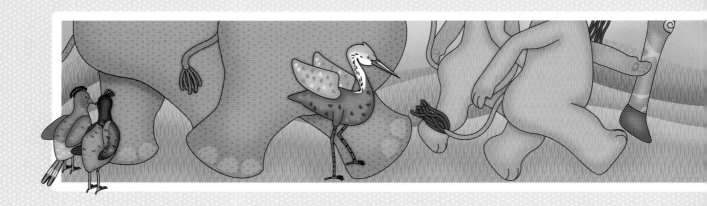

Even the king who sat in the front row.
"Gorillas can't dance," he grumbled out loud.

Then Rick began pounding
a beat for the crowd.

The king wore a stern looking frown on his face,
As the dancers all moved with magnificent grace.

They shuffled and boogied and twisted and spun,
And took a big bow when their dancing was done.

The powerful king didn't speak right away.
Then he grinned ear-to-ear and hollered, "Hurray!

I've watched this performance and feel satisfied.
Gorillas can dance and remain dignified."

The next day the gorillas were snug in their trees.
All of them woke, right along with Louise.
They all heard the drum thump its musical sound.
They all put on dance shoes and hopped to the ground.

The gorillas then moved all their big chubby feet.
They all started rocking along with the beat.
No one was taking a mighty big chance.
The rules now encouraged gorillas to dance.

Louise had a wonderful time for awhile.
She danced by the king and flashed him a smile.

Then Louise did a thing that astonished the king.
She opened her mouth and she started to sing.

Library of Congress Control Number: 2002096528

ISBN 0-9723122-1-8

Printed in Hong Kong

WEE READ PUBLISHING

weereadpublishing.com